The Magic School Bus Rides Again

Attack of the Plants

by
AnnMarie Anderson

BRANCHES

SCHOLASTIC INC.

Ms. Frizzle's Class

Jyoti

Arnold

Ralphie

Wanda

Keesha

Dorothy Ann

Carlos

Tim

TABLE OF CONTENTS

© 2018 Scholastic Inc.
Based on the television series *The Magic School Bus: Rides Again*.
© 2018 MSB Productions, Inc.
Based on the *Magic School Bus* series © Joanna Cole and Bruce Degen.
All rights reserved.

Published by Scholastic Inc., *Publishers since 1920*.
SCHOLASTIC, THE MAGIC SCHOOL BUS, BRANCHES, and logos are trademarks
and/or registered trademarks of Scholastic Inc. All rights reserved.

Library of Congress Cataloging-in-Publication Data available

ISBN 978-1-338-29080-6 (hardcover) / ISBN 978-1-338-29079-0 (paperback)

10 9 8 7 6 5 4 3 2 1   18 19 20 21 22
Printed in China   62

First edition, October 2018
Edited by Marisa Polansky
Book design by Jessica Meltzer

CHAPTER 1

FIRST-DAY SURPRISE

It was the first day of fifth grade at Walkerville Elementary School. Arnold burst into science class and breathed a huge sigh of relief. Everything looked the same as last year.

"Thank goodness!" he said. "I was afraid of what I might find when I got here. Something could have *changed* over the summer!"

"Nope, nothing different," Keesha replied with a smile. "Except Jyoti, of course!"

Keesha gestured to the newest student in their class.

"Hi, Jyoti!" Arnold said. Arnold worried a lot. He liked life best when it was the same as the day before. Still, he could handle *one* new person. "Welcome to your first day. I'll show you around."

"How exciting!" Jyoti said. "From what I've heard about this classroom, I expected things to be a little more, well . . . magical!"

"Don't worry," Arnold replied. "It will be! But first, the normal stuff. Everybody sits in the same place every day, and we all have jobs. It's a delicate balance!"

"Cool," Jyoti replied. "It's like you have your own balanced **ecosystem**."

"According to my research, you're right!" Dorothy Ann chimed in, tapping on her tablet. She prided herself on having an answer for everything. "An ecosystem is—"

"A community of plants and animals, all with a role to play!" Ralphie said.

"So what about me?" Jyoti asked. "Where do I fit in?"

"I don't know yet, but I'm sure we'll find out soon," Arnold said confidently. "You can have Phoebe's old seat. She went back to her old school."

Jyoti was just about to sit when she heard a bus pull up outside.

Honk! Honk!

The kids all rushed to the window to see who it was. Then Jyoti watched in amazement as a yellow school bus landed in front of the school, just like an airplane!

"That's awesome!" Jyoti cried.

"Told you," Arnold replied. "Get ready for the Friz and her mug in"—he glanced at his watch—"14.2 seconds!"

"Ms. Frizzle always gets here at exactly the same time," Wanda explained.

"Yup," Tim agreed. "And she puts the mug that *we* made her . . ."

"In the exact same spot on her desk!" Wanda finished, pointing at the corner of Ms. Frizzle's desk.

The kids all looked around, wondering where Ms. Frizzle would be coming from.

"In three . . . two . . . one," Arnold counted down, looking at his watch. He stopped counting, but Ms. Frizzle hadn't appeared. "That's weird. She's one second late!"

A moment later, a skylight window opened and a woman with red hair and a brightly printed skirt climbed down a rope and into the classroom. She was holding a box of files and the class's pet lizard, Liz.

Arnold gasped in surprise. He took off his glasses, rubbed them on his shirt, and put them on again.

"But *you're* not Ms. Frizzle!" Arnold cried.

"Oh, but I am, Arnold," the woman replied as she placed the file box on her desk. "And I'm very glad you didn't stay home from school today.

"Hey, Tim!" she said enthusiastically. "Love your artwork."

Then she faced Wanda. "How was your summer at the animal rescue?"

The woman whirled around the classroom, saying hello to each student by name.

Finally, she came to Dorothy Ann.

"D.A.!" she greeted her, using her nickname. "According to your research, you must realize that it's—"

"—a whole different Frizzle!" Dorothy Ann exclaimed.

At that moment, the door to the classroom opened, and the original Ms. Frizzle entered the room.

"Ms. Frizzle!" the kids exclaimed in surprise.

"Whoa!" Ralphie replied, looking from one woman to the other. "Total Frizzle overload."

"Actually, you can now call me Professor Frizzle, PhD," the original Ms. Frizzle replied. "It's the first of many changes this year. Class, please welcome your new science teacher—and my little sister—Ms. Fiona Felicity Frizzle!"

CHAPTER 2

NEW DRIVER
AT THE WHEEL

What?!" the kids all shouted in surprise.

"This can't be happening," Arnold moaned.

The new Ms. Frizzle smiled and headed over to her desk. She hunted through her file box and pulled out a potted plant.

"Hmmm . . ." she wondered, looking around the room. "Now, where do I put my magical, crazy-growing, must-stay-in-a-pot Frizzleium vine? How about . . . here!"

She placed the plant firmly in the spot on the desk where Professor Frizzle's mug used to go.

"What?!" gasped Arnold. "But, but, but . . . no!"

Arnold's protests were drowned out by Professor Frizzle.

"Now, there's so much to do today, kids!" she said. "To the bus!"

As everyone raced out of the classroom, Arnold dashed to the desk and grabbed the plant.

"New teacher or not, that plant does *not* belong in the special spot," he said, shaking his head. Then he slipped the plant into his backpack and headed outside to the bus.

The class gathered around Professor Frizzle in the school parking lot.

"My sensational sister will be taking over this year—with Liz's help, of course!" Professor Frizzle said proudly.

"But what about *you*?" Wanda asked. She was always concerned with the well-being of other people and animals.

"As a research professor, I'll be traveling the universe!" Professor Frizzle replied.

"But what about *us*?" Tim asked. "We need to be taking chances!"

"And making mistakes!" Keesha added. Professor Frizzle was definitely not the average teacher. She loved taking her students on amazing field trips on her magic school bus, and she always encouraged them to be adventurous and daring when it came to studying science.

"Yeah!" Wanda exclaimed. "And getting messy!"

"Oh, don't worry," Professor Frizzle chuckled. "You'll be getting plenty of that."

As if to prove her older sister's point, the new Ms. Frizzle raced over to the bus.

"Bus, do your stuff!" she said confidently, but the bus didn't budge. "Hmmm . . . something's missing."

"Fiona!" Professor Frizzle called, holding out a key ring to her younger sister. "You forgot the keys."

"Thanks, Sis!" Ms. Frizzle said, smiling. "Come along now, everyone."

The kids all ran to the bus and climbed aboard.

"I wonder where we're going," Ralphie said.

"It's a mystery!" Ms. Frizzle said. "Don't you love it?"

"Yay!" Dorothy Ann yelled. "A field trip!"

But Arnold was less than excited. He sat down next to Jyoti and groaned. The bus had gotten an update, too.

"Even my seat is different," he grumbled. "I had gotten it all worked in and everything."

"Seat belts, everyone!" Ms. Frizzle cried as she fired up the bus.

Arnold buckled up, looked out the window, and waved good-bye to Professor Frizzle with a sigh.

Ms. Frizzle studied the dashboard. "So many modes to choose from," she said. "But which one do we pick? There we go!"

She pressed a button, and the bus launched into the air.

"Whoa!" the kids cried as the bus rocked from side to side.

"So cool!" Jyoti exclaimed. She was all smiles, despite the rough ride.

"I'm guessing you don't get motion sick much," Arnold said.

Suddenly, the bus landed with a *thud*.

"We're here!" Ms. Frizzle exclaimed.

"Good," Arnold said. He unbuckled his seat belt and headed for the door. "Because I cannot get off this bus fast enough!"

He was about to step outside when he realized the bus was teetering on top of a cliff, hundreds of feet above the ground. But before he could scoot backward, Arnold lost his balance.

"Whoooooaaaa!" Arnold cried as he fell out the door. "Help!"

CHAPTER 3

ISLAND ADVENTURE

Ms. Frizzle pushed a button on the dashboard, and a robotic arm appeared from the side of the bus.

"Hang in there, Arnold!" she cried as the arm grabbed Arnold by the waistband of his pants and dropped him back inside the bus. "I haven't lost a kid yet!"

"Oh, sure," Arnold groaned as he adjusted his pants. "She may be new, but she already knows how to work the robotic wedgie arm."

Suddenly, the bus began to wobble.

"You know," Carlos said, peeking out the window, looking at the cliff below. "She seems nice and everything, but I'm not sure about her parking skills."

The kids heard a creaking sound as the rocks under the bus's wheels gave way. A second later, the bus tumbled right over the edge!

"Ahhhhhhh!" the kids cried.

Luckily, Ms. Frizzle hit another button on the dashboard, and the bus soon floated back up to the top of the cliff.

"How much do I love this bus?" she squealed. "Phew!" Tim said with relief when they were back on solid ground. "That was close."

"That was exciting!" Ms. Frizzle said. "Since we're here—wherever that is—we might as well look around, right?"

"She doesn't even know where we are?" Arnold whispered as he and the others followed Ms. Frizzle outside.

Dorothy Ann pushed a few buttons on her tablet.

"According to my research, we're in the Galápagos Islands," she said as a park ranger suddenly jumped out from behind some bushes.

"Fiona!" the ranger cried. "How are you doing?"

"Galápagos Gil!" Ms. Frizzle said. "What's up, bear man?"

"They know each other?" Keesha asked.

"Well, like a lot of the animals here, the only place you find Galápagos Gil is on the Galápagos Islands!" Ms. Frizzle replied.

"Everything here lives in perfect balance. Look at this healthy, special ecosystem!" said Galápagos Gil.

He gestured to the plants and animals all around him as he led the class down a path. Meanwhile, Tim stepped closer to his teacher.

"You know, Ms. Frizzle," he said, "whenever we used to go on a field trip, Professor Frizzle used to—how can I put this?—**enhance** the experience!"

"Ah, with sandwiches?" Ms. Frizzle asked.

"No, with magic!" the kids all shouted.

"I *knew* you were going to say that!" the Friz replied.

She took out her magical remote control and pressed a few buttons. There was a swirl of sparkles, and suddenly Carlos turned into a giant tortoise and Wanda transformed into a finch! Then Ms. Frizzle pushed a few more buttons, and the other kids found themselves wearing magic glasses.

"Nice!" the kids cried. When they looked through their new glasses, they saw glowing green arrows pointing from some plants and animals to other plants and animals.

"The glasses show you how the different parts of the ecosystem fit together," Dorothy Ann said.

"There are arrows pointing from mushrooms to grasshoppers to owls," Tim said. "What does that mean?"

"Look at Carlos and Wanda," Dorothy Ann explained. "Plants grow, tortoises eat their leaves, ticks bite the tortoises, and finches eat the ticks!"

Tortoise Carlos munched on a mouthful of leaves.

"Mmm," he said. "These are actually pretty good!"

Finch Wanda nibbled on some of the ticks on Carlos's neck.

"The kid in me says ewww," she said, "but the finch in me says yum, yum, yum!"

The kids all laughed.

"Everything here is **interconnected**," Jyoti exclaimed.

"You nailed it, new kid!" Ms. Frizzle said to Jyoti. "Everything has a role to play, and that keeps everything stable. And since this is an island by itself in the middle of the ocean, it has its own natural balance!"

Ms. Frizzle pushed a few buttons on the remote control, and the glasses disappeared. But Carlos and Wanda were still in animal form!

"Come along, everyone!" Ms. Frizzle said.

"Uh, Ms. Frizzle?" Tortoise Carlos asked nervously. "What about us?!"

CHAPTER 4

BOOTING UP

"Oh! Of course!" Ms. Frizzle said. Then she pressed a button on the remote control, and Carlos changed into—a horse?

"Nope, that's not right," Ms. Frizzle muttered. She pressed again and again, and he and Wanda turned into an elephant and a mouse, a hippo and a chipmunk, and a lemur and a hen. "Oh, I love this thing! Just say when!"

A second later, the kids were Carlos and Wanda again.

"When!" they both shouted.

"Aw," Jyoti groaned, disappointed. "I wanted her to keep going!"

As the kids followed Galápagos Gil and Ms. Frizzle, Tim had a sudden thought.

"Galápagos Gil?" he asked. "With everything in **unison**, don't you worry about something throwing that off?"

"You bet your giant tortoise we do!" Galápagos Gil replied. "That's why we inspect everything."

Galápagos Gil led them to the airport terminal building, where travelers were arriving by plane.

"You mean like luggage, coats, hats—everything?!" Keesha asked in surprise.

"Everything," Galápagos Gil replied, nodding and pointing to some workers who were inspecting and brushing the soles of travelers' shoes as they passed through the airport. "We don't want any new plants or animals to get here. Accidents happen, you know."

"Accidents?" Tim asked. "So you have to look at everything *really* close up."

Ms. Frizzle gasped in delight.

"Tim, what a great idea!" she exclaimed, and she pulled out the remote control again.

"Oh no," Arnold groaned.

With the click of a button, Ms. Frizzle had shrunk down herself and the entire class—including Galápagos Gil—so they were smaller than ants!

"Wahoo!" she cried. "I love getting **microscopic**."

"That was so magical!" Jyoti cried. She could hardly contain her excitement. "Majorly magical!"

"Sure," Arnold agreed, pointing to an ant looming over them. "Until you get eaten!"

But the ant had other things on its mind.

Ms. Frizzle led her students to a pair of hiking boots in the grass. They looked enormous compared to the microscopic class.

"Let's suit up to boot up!" she called, and with one click of the remote, the class was outfitted from head to toe in rock-climbing gear. They raced toward the boot that was lying on its side and began to climb up the sole.

"I'm rock climbing . . . on a boot!" Jyoti said.

"Okay, look closely, everyone," Ms. Frizzle reminded them. "Anything could be an **invasive** species that throws off the island's delicate balance."

Dorothy Ann looked up from the enormous speck of soil she was studying. "Is an invasive species a plant or an animal the island's not ready for?" she asked.

"Yes to the guess from D.A.!" Ms. Frizzle replied enthusiastically. "If things that already live here have no defense, the new species can take over and change everything!"

"And change everything," Arnold mumbled grumpily. "I know what *that's* like."

"There's a lot of dirt on these boots," Keesha pointed out. "Looks like he's been hiking in the woods back in his home country."

"Well, let's hope there were no invasive hitchhikers!" Ms. Frizzle replied.

Arnold took a step forward, but his foot got stuck in the muck.

"Ahhh!" he cried as he fell facedown in some dirt, and then a bug crawled out.

"We have insects!" Carlos announced.

Arnold got to his feet but stumbled a second time. This time, he landed in a glob of mud that was covered in tiny white dots.

"And those look like insect eggs," Jyoti pointed out.

"Jyoti, you're right!" Ms. Frizzle exclaimed. "These insect eggs could mean the unwelcome arrival of a whole family of gypsy moths."

"And we don't want that!" Dorothy Ann gasped, pulling up some images on her tablet. "Here's what they can do."

She showed her friends a photo of a healthy, green forest. Then she showed them a photo of the same forest after gypsy moths had been there. The leaves on the trees had completely disappeared! They had been eaten by the gypsy moths.

"That poor ecosystem," Wanda said, shaking her head. "It was totally defenseless against the invasive species. What do we do now? We can't let those moth eggs enter the ecosystem!"

CHAPTER 5

AN INVASIVE... TEACHER?

Luckily, an airport inspector noticed the moth eggs, too. Ms. Frizzle zapped the kids back to normal size as the inspector questioned the tourist.

Arnold was happy to be regular-sized again, but he was still very unhappy about their new teacher.

"Ralphie," he whispered. "Are you thinking what I'm thinking?"

"I think so," Ralphie said. "But how would we get pizza delivery here?"

"No!" Arnold groaned. "I'm thinking the new Ms. Frizzle keeps talking about invasive species because she *is* one."

"Relax, buddy," Ralphie said. "She's got a sense of humor. I can work with that."

"Don't you get it?" Arnold asked, frustrated. "It's part of her plot! Our classroom is a perfectly balanced ecosystem, like these islands. We need to protect it!"

Wanda overheard the last part of their conversation.

"Arnold, what are you doing?" she asked.

"Just protecting our ecosystem from an invasive teacher, that's all!" he shouted dramatically. Then he stormed off, feeling misunderstood. Why couldn't his friends see what was going on?

Arnold noticed that the others were busy listening to Galápagos Gil, so he snuck back to the bus and grabbed his backpack, which contained Ms. Frizzle's potted plant. He carried it back outside and placed it on a giant rock.

"There!" he said happily. "This plant definitely does *not* belong in our classroom ecosystem."

As if in response, the plant suddenly started . . . walking?

"Hey?" Arnold said, realizing he had placed the plant on the back of a giant tortoise. "Actually, it looks good on you. It matches your shell!"

Arnold quickly hurried back to the bus. He didn't see the plant slip off the tortoise's back and fall to the ground, shattering the clay pot.

Meanwhile, the other kids were already back in their seats on the bus.

"All aboard, class!" Ms. Frizzle said as Arnold climbed up the steps. Then she pressed a few buttons on the dashboard. "Bus, undo your stuff!"

The bus whirled and twirled and magically **transported** the class back to Walkerville Elementary School. Meanwhile, Ms. Frizzle's magical, crazy-growing, must-stay-in-a-pot Frizzleium vine was busy growing in a really crazy way!

CHAPTER 6

TIME-TRAVELING TOURISTS

Back at school, Professor Frizzle was packing her banana-yellow motorbike for one of her research trips when the Magic School Bus reappeared in the parking lot. Arnold walked over to his former teacher.

"Uh, Ms. Friz—I mean, Professor Frizzle?" he asked nervously.

"Hi, Arnold," Professor Frizzle replied as a golden tamarind monkey hopped onto Arnold's shoulders. "Meet my new research assistant, Goldie! What can we do for you?"

"Um, I'm not sure how to say this, but you need to come back!" he begged.

"What's the problem?" Professor Frizzle asked.

"Your sister is nice and everything, but she's new!" Arnold said.

"Yes?" Professor Frizzle said, raising her eyebrows.

"And new things are always trouble!" Arnold continued. "Like on the Galápagos. Something new could totally upset their whole ecosystem!"

"True, sometimes a new species can be a problem," Professor Frizzle explained as a bee buzzed around her head. "But not always! Honeybees were new to North America once. But they became part of a new balance. They didn't bring on a disaster at all—they just brought yummy honey!"

"So ecosystems can create a new balance over time, and it's not always bad?" Arnold asked.

"That's right," Professor Frizzle replied. "Sometimes it works out wonderfully, like with the honeybee. But with invasive species, it's not so good."

"I wish I knew how it was going to work out for our class," Arnold said sadly.

"Maybe a little magic will help you figure that out," Professor Frizzle said with a twinkle in her eye.

"Magic?" Arnold asked eagerly.

"It runs in our family, you know," said Professor Frizzle, smiling.

"Thanks, Ms. Frizzle," Arnold said. "I mean, *Professor* Frizzle."

Then he hurried inside the school and back to science class. Ms. Frizzle greeted him warmly.

"Hey, Arnold," she said. "I see one of my students hasn't **adapted** to the idea of a new teacher."

"I'm supposed to ask you about magic," Arnold replied, scratching his head in confusion. "But I don't see how that's going to help me see how things will work out in the future."

"Well, let's go see!" Ms. Frizzle replied.

"Are you saying we should go ahead in *time*?" Arnold asked in surprise.

"Well, there's no better time to visit the future than the present!" Ms. Frizzle said, winking. "To the bus!"

The kids followed Ms. Frizzle and Arnold outside and climbed aboard. A few seconds later, they were being transported through a time tunnel. They soon arrived in the science classroom of the future in miniature form, which was perfect for making observations while remaining unnoticed.

"Wow!" Jyoti exclaimed. "Look at all that cool technology. I want to go to this school thirty years in the future."

Ralphie didn't look as excited.

"If I don't get my grades up I *will* be at this school thirty years from now!" he joked.

"Look!" Keesha exclaimed as she pointed out the kids in the future class. "It's Arnold Junior, Wanda Junior, Ralphie Junior—everybody Junior!"

"See, Arnold," Ms. Frizzle said reassuringly. "The class's ecosystem has survived. There's nothing to worry about!"

"You're right!" Arnold exclaimed. "What a relief! I guess I was totally overreacting."

Suddenly, Wanda Junior started talking.

"Guys, want to see my project on the huge Galápagos crisis?" she asked.

"Crisis in the Galápagos?" Arnold asked in alarm. "What is she talking about?"

CHAPTER 7

DOUBLE INVASION

To the bus!" Ms. Frizzle cried. "We'd better head back to the Galápagos to find out."

The kids hurried back aboard, and the bus took off. As they approached the Galápagos Islands, they saw a green vine with pink flowers growing everywhere.

"Oh no, no, no!" Arnold cried. "This can't be happening!"

"Arnold, are you okay?" Jyoti asked.

"That plant is growing everywhere," Wanda said.

"We can barely see where we're going!" Carlos added as he looked out the window at the thick green vines.

Finally, the bus landed in a bare patch of earth. The kids climbed out and began exploring. All around them, the only things they could see were green vines and pink flowers!

"These poor islands," Wanda said sadly.

"Well, at least it can't get any worse," Arnold noted, trying to look on the bright side.

"Oh no!" Carlos exclaimed. "It *is* worse!"

Suddenly, the kids were surrounded by hundreds of rabbits. The furry creatures nibbled constantly on the green vines growing all around them.

"This is not good!" Arnold groaned.

"It is a rather *hare*-raising situation," Ms. Frizzle joked.

"Bunnies!" Wanda cried. "They're adorable. This is the best thing ever!"

There was a rustling sound in the vines, and a park ranger appeared.

"Galápagos Gil?" Wanda asked. "Is that really you?"

"The Second," he replied. "You must be the Frizzle class. My dad told me you might show up one of these days."

"Indeed we did!" Ms. Frizzle said, smiling. "So, what caused this?"

"No one knows," Gil replied, shaking his head. "But somehow this plant wound up on these islands and threw off our ecosystem."

"What's with all the bunnies?" Arnold asked.

"Well, when the plants started taking over, some people tried to control the plants," Gil replied. "So they brought in bunnies to eat the vine."

"But there was nothing to control the bunnies?" Carlos guessed.

"Exactly!" Gil concluded. "So now we have two invasive species instead of one."

"That plant is obviously a **non-native** invasive species," Dorothy Ann said. "But what is it?"

Ms. Frizzle examined one of the plant's leaves closely.

"Aha!" she cried. "I know exactly what it is! That's the magical, crazy-growing, must-stay-in-a-pot Frizzleium vine."

"Like the one you put on your desk in the past?" Tim asked.

"Exactly!" Ms. Frizzle said. "Only how did it get here? Did I cause this? That would have been a terrible thing to do!"

"I'm sure it's not that bad," Arnold said.

"Oh, but it is, Arnold!" Ms. Frizzle explained, sobbing. "This is a really big mistake. I'm supposed to lead by example! And if it was my fault, I don't know what I'll do!"

"It *is* an example," Arnold said. "Um, of a plant, growing like crazy. And taking over the islands."

"Well, maybe I *am* an invasive species," Ms. Frizzle said to Arnold. "Maybe I shouldn't be here. Should I ask my sister to come back?"

"I—I, uh, I mean, you shouldn't take it so hard," Arnold said. "But still, getting old Friz back? That would be amazing, huh?"

"Arnold, no!" the other kids cried.

CHAPTER 8

FREE-FALLING

Ms. Frizzle looked at Arnold carefully.

"That settles it," she said, and she pulled out her cell phone. "I'm calling my sister right now."

"Woo-hoooooo!" Professor Frizzle answered the phone.

"Hey, Sis," Ms. Frizzle replied. "Did I catch you at a bad time?"

"Not at all," Professor Frizzle replied. "What's up?"

"Listen, I really messed up," Ms. Frizzle began. "You see, what happened was—"

"Wait!" Arnold shouted, cutting off Ms. Frizzle. "Um, can I talk to the professor? Privately?"

The other kids quickly stepped aside to give Arnold some space.

"You've got it!" Ms. Frizzle replied, and she pressed a button on her phone. Suddenly, Arnold was zapped with a burst of magical sparkles. A second later, he was hundreds of miles above Earth, free-falling through the air next to a skydiving Professor Frizzle!

"Ahhhhhh!" Arnold cried.

"Hi, Arnold!" the professor greeted him as if they were chatting over cheeseburgers. "What's on your mind?"

"Uh, right," Arnold said quickly. "There's an invasive plant species in the Galápagos and it was my fault. I did it. I left it on the island."

"Goodness!" Professor Frizzle exclaimed. "Why in the sky would you do that?"

"That plant in place of your mug on your old desk—well, it was just too much," Arnold replied. "I know I'm the guy who hates change. But I caused the biggest change ever, in the form of plants and bunnies. Can you help us fix this?"

"Remember when I said a little magic would help?" Professor Frizzle asked.

"Yes, that's it!" Arnold shouted. "Magic bunny-disappearing spray!"

Professor Frizzle chuckled.

"No, Arnold," she replied.

"Wait, the best way to stop an invasive species is to not let it invade in the first place!" Arnold exclaimed.

"Exactly!" Professor Frizzle said proudly. "Good thinking, Arnold. Well, maybe you'd better get back now."

Then she pulled a cord, and her parachute unfolded. Just as Arnold realized he wasn't even wearing a parachute, another burst of magical sparkles surrounded him. A moment later, he was back on the Galápagos Islands. He landed in front of Ms. Frizzle and his classmates with a *thud*.

"Arnold, hey!" Ms. Frizzle said.

Arnold stood up and brushed himself off.

"Ms. Frizzle, you didn't leave the plant here," he told her, hanging his head. "I did."

"What?" the other kids gasped in surprise.

"But I know how to fix it!" Arnold said apologetically. "We just have to take the plant away *before* it can cause any trouble."

"To the bus?" Ms. Frizzle asked everyone.

"To the bus!" Arnold cried, racing ahead of everyone.

In the blink of an eye, the bus had transported the entire class back to the Galápagos Islands in the present day. Arnold jumped off the bus. He hurried to the spot where he had left the plant, but he didn't see it anywhere.

"I left it right here," he said, scratching his head. A moment later, the tortoise appeared, the plant balanced on its shell.

"Tortoise!" Arnold cried. "Wait up!"

But at that moment, the plant slipped off the tortoise's back. It landed with a loud *crash*, and the pot shattered into pieces.

"Uh-oh," Arnold said as the vine stretched out its green **tendrils** and started to grow. "Noooooooooo!"

CHAPTER 9

A NEW BALANCE

Arnold threw himself on top of the vine, grabbing one of the green tendrils. But the plant was growing so quickly he couldn't stop it! The other kids quickly hopped off the bus.

"Hang on, Arnold!" Jyoti cried.

"We're coming to help you!" Tim yelled.

The plant was out of control. One tendril had wrapped itself around Arnold's body, while another tendril was slapping his face.

"It's okay, Arnold," Wanda shouted as she and the others ran toward him. "We're coming!"

Jyoti delivered a strong roundhouse kick to the plant, while the other kids each grabbed a tendril. Arnold managed to get free, and he grabbed two tendrils.

"Gotcha!" he shouted as he tried to get the vine under control. "This . . . plant . . . is . . . going . . . crazy!"

As the kids fought the plant, Ms. Frizzle calmly pulled out a new clay pot. Then she held it under the plant, and some magic sparkles appeared. Suddenly, the plant began to shrink as it was sucked into its new pot.

"Awesome!" Jyoti exclaimed. "Best class ever!"

"Thank you, Ms. Frizzle," Arnold said.

"No, thank you, Arnold," she replied, smiling at him. "Because of you, the carefully balanced ecosystem here will stay balanced! You know what, Mr. Perlstein? You're all right."

"You know what, Ms. Frizzle?" Arnold replied. "So are you!"

A short bus ride later, Ms. Frizzle's class was back in the science classroom at Walkerville Elementary.

"Ah," Arnold sighed as he went over to his desk. "It's good to see you, old, familiar desk and old, familiar pencil case!"

Then he walked up to Ms. Frizzle, who was busy settling into her new desk.

"And it's good to have a new teacher," he said. "One who's good new, like a honeybee."

Arnold's classmates looked confused, but Ms. Frizzle understood.

"Hmmm," she said. "Where should my plant go?"

Arnold took the plant from her and placed it on the corner of the desk right where Professor Frizzle's mug used to go.

"There you go," he said proudly. "The place of honor."

"Ah, perfect!" Ms. Frizzle exclaimed. "Thank you, Arnold."

Jyoti stepped up to the desk and slipped a high-tech dish underneath the pot.

"It's a little something I made," she explained. "It has a motion-sensor. That way if this little guy starts roaming again, we'll know."

"Nice," Ralphie said. "Looks like the new kid just found her spot in the class ecosystem."

Suddenly, Professor Frizzle and Goldie appeared at the window. They were riding her banana-yellow motorbike, which hovered magically in mid-air.

"I like it!" the professor exclaimed. "New gear, new teacher, new balance! You're going to have great new adventures, class! I just have one thing left to say to you . . ."

"What is it?" Tim asked, curious.

"Wahoooo!" Professor Frizzle replied as her motorbike zoomed off on an amazing adventure of her own.

"Wahoooo!" the class said, and waved good-bye to their old teacher.

GLOSSARY

Adapt: to change because you are in a new situation

Ecosystem: a community of plants and animals that affect one another

Enhance: improve

Interconnected: joined together or linked in some way

Invasive: a plant or disease that spreads or grows in a harmful way

Microscopic: too small to be seen without a microscope

Non-native: not originally from a particular place

Tendrils: leaves or stems that attach a climbing plant to its support

Transport: to move from one place to another

Unison: Occuring at the same time; together

Ask Professor Frizzle

Nature doesn't have fences to keep animals in their own ecosystems, so what's stopping one from invading all on its own?

 Wild animals do roam free inside boundaries like oceans and mountains. But they like to stay in places that have what they need to survive. It could be a small range, like one tiny island. Or it might be all the oceans in the world.

Okay. So invasive species make a mess. But what if you don't have a time machine? How do you fix it after the fact?

It's hard to undo damage done. But we can stop invasive species in the first place. For example, never set pets free in the wild. And when you travel, be careful not to bring stowaways!

Do we all play a part in the ecosystem? Even me?

Even you! All species have specific roles to play in keeping the ecosystem in balance and humans are no different! It's up to us to work together with the plants and animals to keep our earth healthy.

Professor Frizzle, will the environment change a lot in the future?

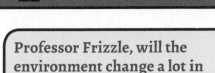

The environment changes steadily over time! But luckily, scientists are always coming up with new technology to help us understand our surroundings as we adapt.

Thanks for answering our questions, Professor Frizzle. Where will you be the next time I want your advice?

Wherever the wind takes me. Woo-hooooooo!

The Magic School Bus Rides Again

QUESTIONS and ACTIVITIES

1. Ms. Frizzle turns Carlos and Wanda into a giant tortoise and a finch to show how the animals are connected. Can you think of two other animals that rely on each other?

2. Draw a picture of the plants and animals that live in your ecosystem. Add arrows to show how the different members work together.

3. Ms. Frizzle shrinks the kids so they can investigate a dirty boot. If you could become tiny, what would you investigate and why?

4. How do you think Arnold felt when he realized the trouble he had caused by bringing Ms. Frizzle's plant into the Galápagos Islands?

5. Arnold isn't a big fan of change. What is one change in your life that you've had to overcome? How did you get through it?